I Can Dress Myself

By ANNA H. DICKSON • Illustrated by CAROL NICKLAUS

A SESAME STREET / GOLDEN BOOK

Published by Western Publishing Company, Inc.
in conjunction with Children's Television Workshop.

I can dress myself.

I can button my underwear.

I can snap my shirt.

I can zip up my blue jeans.

I can buckle my belt.

I can put on my socks.

I can pull on my boots.

I can hook my vest.

I can tie my bandanna.

I can put on my jacket.

I can pin on my badge.

I can put on my hat.

Oh, I am so proud!

I can dress myself.